Sandnado

Owlkids Books

Chirp, Tweet, and Squawk loved to play in their playhouse. On this particular day, they were playing…

"Desert explorers!" suggested Tweet.

"Thirsty desert explorers!" added Squawk.

"Thirsty desert explorers lost in the hottest desert on the planet!" continued Chirp.

"The bad news is, we've run out of water," said Explorer Tweet.

"The good news is, I see trees over there!" said Explorer Chirp.

"Well, I have news, too," said Explorer Squawk. *"We can't drink trees!"*

"Trees mean that there's an oasis up ahead," said Explorer Tweet.

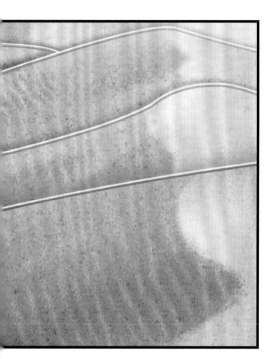

"What's an oasis?" asked Squawk.

"An oasis is a place where plants and trees grow in the desert," said Tweet.

"And where there are trees, there's water!" said Chirp.

"That is the *best* news ever!" said Squawk.

"Unfortunately," said Chirp, "more bad news is heading our way…"

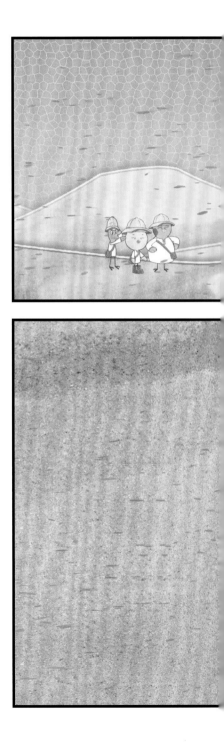

Suddenly, out of nowhere came a strong, sandy wind.

"It's a sandstorm!" yelled Chirp.

"What's a sandstorm?" asked Squawk.

"It's a storm with sand in it!" yelled Tweet.

"Ack! Now my mouth has sand in it!" yelled Squawk. *"I can't drink sand!"*

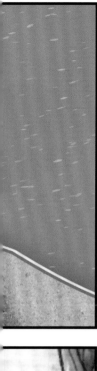

"It's hard to see where we're going!" said Chirp. "Stick together, you guys!"

"How are we going to get out of this?" asked Squawk.

"Maybe there's something in my super-handy explorer pack that'll help," said Tweet.

"Good idea! Look in the box—I mean, your pack—with all the helpful stuff," said Chirp.

The three friends opened the lid and looked inside.

"What about rubber bands…some tin foil… or a wooden spoon?" asked Tweet.

"None of those will help," said Chirp.

"What about this umbrella?" asked Squawk.

"Hmm, an umbrella shields you from the rain or the sun," said Tweet.

"I bet it can shield us from sand, too!" said Chirp.

Back in the desert, explorers Chirp, Tweet, and Squawk needed to escape the sandstorm to reach the oasis...

"Quick, Chirp! Press the button on the umbrella!" yelled Squawk.

"Umbrella activated!" yelled Chirp.

"It's working!" said Tweet. "The umbrella is shielding us from the sand!"

But as the explorers carefully made their way toward the oasis, the wind got stronger...

"This isn't just a sandstorm!" said Chirp.

"What is it? A tornado?" asked Tweet.

"It's worse than a tornado," said Chirp. "It's a...a..."

"Sandnado!" yelled Squawk. "A GIANT SANDNADO!"

The giant sandnado was sucking up everything in its path.

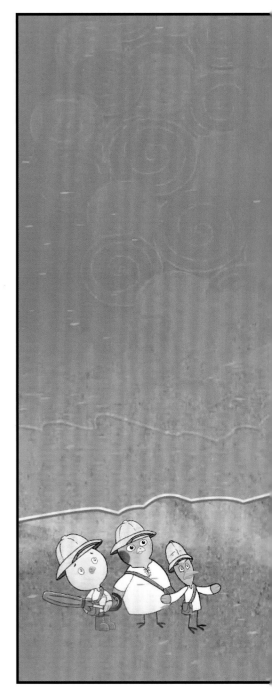

"Whoaaa! The sandnado is picking us up!" said Chirp.

"Whoaaa! The sandnado is spinning us around!" said Tweet.

"Whoaaa! The sandnado is making me dizzy!" said Squawk.

"We need to use the umbrella again!" yelled Chirp. "Everybody grab on to it!"

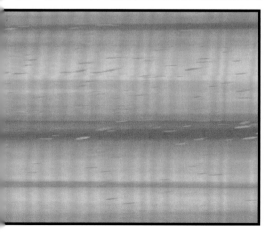

"I get to push the button this time!" yelled Squawk.

Explorers Chirp, Tweet, and Squawk used the umbrella to fly up and out of the sandnado.

"We're flying!" said Squawk.

"Well, it's more like we're floating," said Tweet.

"The good news is, we're floating right into the oasis!" said Chirp.

"The even better news is, there's plenty of water!" said Tweet.

"*I can totally drink water!*" said Squawk. "That is the *greatest* news ever!"

From an episode of the animated TV series *Chirp*, produced by Sinking Ship (Chirp) Productions. Based on the Chirp character created by Bob Kain.

Based on the TV episode *Sandnado* written by Diana Moore. Story adaptation written by J. Torres.

CHIRP and the CHIRP character are trademarks of Bayard Presse Canada Inc.

Text © 2016 Owlkids Books Inc.
Interior illustrations by Smiley Guy Studios. © 2016 Sinking Ship (Chirp) Productions. Used under license.
Cover illustration by Cale Atkinson, based on images from the TV episode. Cover illustration © 2016 Owlkids Books Inc.

Owlkids Books acknowledges the financial support of the Canada Council for the Arts, the Ontario Arts Council, the Government of Canada through the Canada Book Fund (CBF) and the Government of Ontario through the Ontario Media Development Corporation's Book Initiative for our publishing activities.

Published in Canada by
Owlkids Books Inc.
10 Lower Spadina Avenue
Toronto, ON M5V 2Z2

Cataloguing data available from Library and Archives Canada.

ISBN 978-1-77147-185-5

Edited by: Jennifer Stokes
Designed by: Susan Sinclair

Canadä

Manufactured in Shenzhen, China, in September 2015, by C&C Joint Printing Co.
Job #HP4362

A   B   C   D   E   F

Publisher of Chirp, chickaDEE and OWL
www.owlkidsbooks.com

Owlkids Books is a division of Bayard CANADA